3 1994 01539 2977

SANTA ANA PUBLIC LIBRARY
NOV - 5 2015

D0518083

SPY GUY

THE NOT-SO-SECRET AGENT

by Jessica Young

Illustrated by Charles Santoso

Houghton Mifflin Harcourt

Boston • New York

J PICT BK YOUNG, J.
Young, Jessica
Spy Guy

$16.99
CENTRAL   31994015392977

For Wesley and Clara, my favorite little spies —J.Y.
For Pa, Ma, Bro, Sis, & Jen —C.S.

Text copyright © 2015 by Jessica Young • Illustrations copyright © 2015 by Charles Santoso • All rights reserved. For information about permission to reproduce selections from this book, write to Permissions, Houghton Mifflin Harcourt Publishing Company, 215 Park Avenue South, New York, New York 10003. • www.hmhco.com • The illustrations in this book were painted digitally. • The text type was set in Plumsky Black. • The display type was set in Pink Broccoli. • Library of Congress Cataloging-in-Publication Data: Young, Jessica (Jessica E.), author.   Spy Guy / by Jessica Young ; Illustrated by Charles Santoso.   pages cm   Summary: Spy Guy is determined to become a good, sneaky spy, but he cannot do it without the help of his father, the Chief.   ISBN 978-0-544-20859-9   [1. Spies—Fiction. 2. Perseverance (Ethics)—Fiction. 3. Fathers and sons—Fiction. 4. Humorous stories.] I. Santoso, Charles, illustrator. II. Title.   PZ7.Y8657Spy 2015   [E]—dc23
2014015877 • Manufactured in China
SCP 10 9 8 7 6 5 4 3 2 1
4500517860

Spy Guy was a spy.

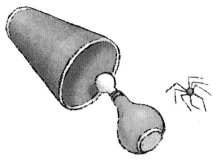

But not a very good one.

Spies are sneaky.
Not Spy Guy.

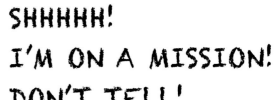

SHHHHH!
I'M ON A MISSION!
DON'T TELL!

He needed help.

So Spy Guy went to
Headquarters to see the Chief.
"Chief!" he said. "Tell me the secret to spying!"

"Spy Guy," said the Chief,
"*that* you must discover
for yourself. But if you
seek to sneak,
try not to speak."

Spy Guy was careful not to speak
as he tiptoed down the street.
But he didn't get far before . . .

SQUEAK!

SQUEAK! SQUEAK!

Spy Guy went back
to the Chief.

"Chief!" he said.
"When I try to sneak,
my shoes squeak!"

"Spy Guy," said the Chief,
"great sneakers need great sneakers."

Spy Guy put on his
brand-new shoes.
He didn't make a sound
as he crept through town.
But . . .

everyone saw him coming.

Spy Guy visited the Chief again.
"Chief!" he said. "When I'm sneaking, everyone is peeking."

"So I see," said the Chief. "When spying, it is wise
to wear a good disguise."

Spy Guy put on some camouflage.
He felt pretty sneaky
as he slunk through the trees.
But suddenly, he had to . . .

A-A-ACHOOO

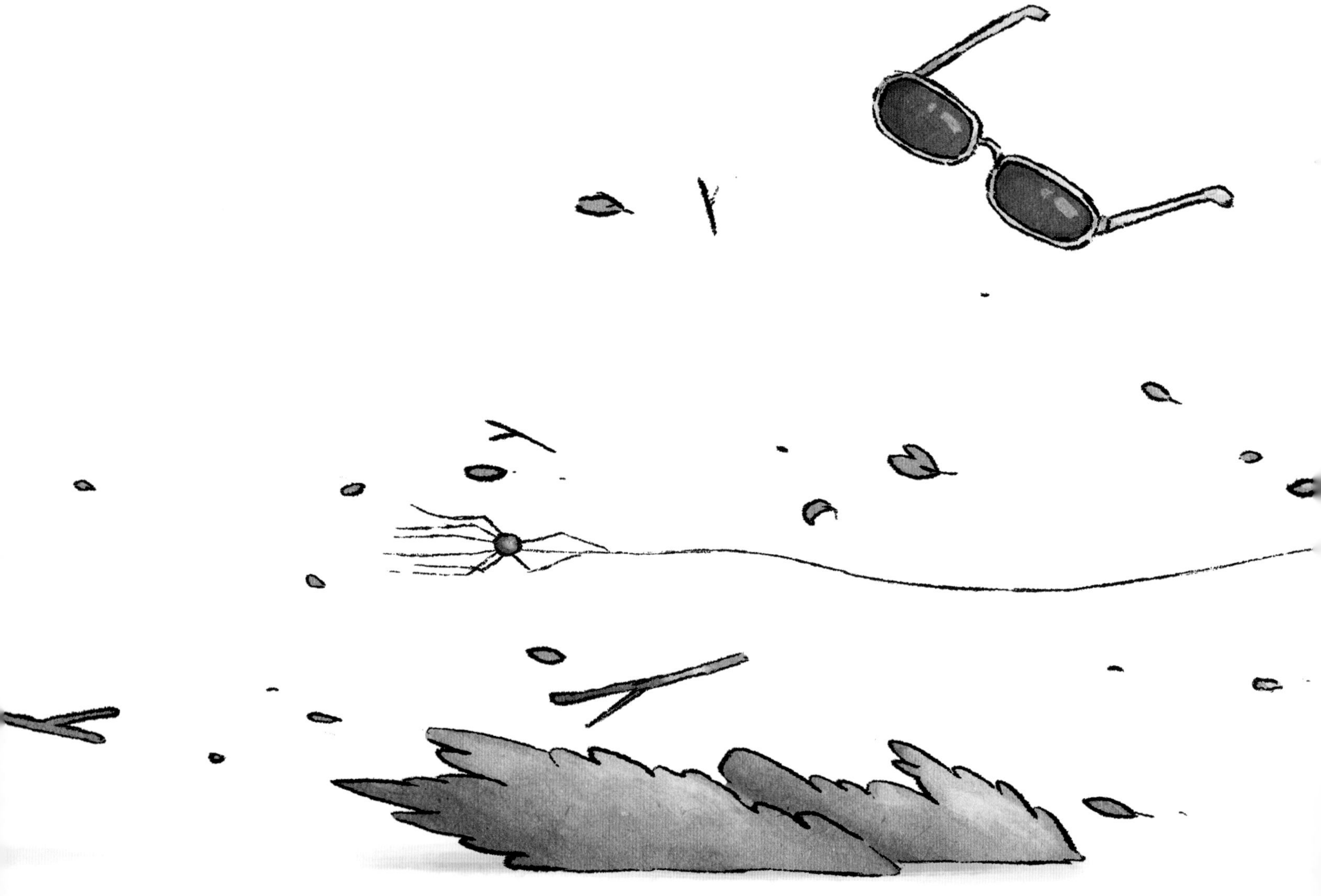

Spy Guy returned to the Chief.
"Chief!" he said. "When I try to
sneak, I sneeze!"

"Spy Guy," said the Chief,
"if you want to be stealthy,
first you must be healthy."

So Spy Guy gobbled down a
big bowl of soup.

SLURP! SLURP!

"Wait!" said the Chief.
"If you slurp, you will . . ."

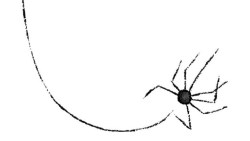

Spy Guy went to see the Chief one last time.
"Chief!" he said.
"I've done everything you said, but I still can't sneak! Please tell me the secret to spying!"

"If you can sneak up on me,"
said the Chief,
"then you will know."

Spy Guy tried.

After a while, he was exhausted.

But just as he was about to quit . . .

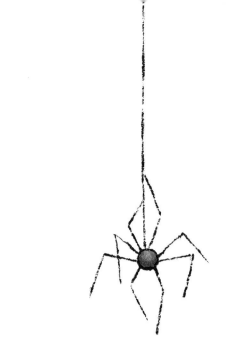

"Very sneaky, Spy Guy," said the Chief.

"The secret to spying," said Spy Guy,
"is never stop trying!"

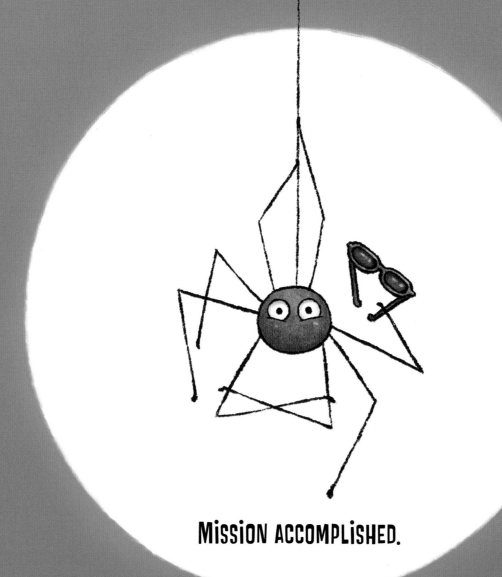

MISSION ACCOMPLISHED.